It Takes Two to
T'wit T'woo

Published by Bonney Press,
an imprint of Hinkler Books Pty Ltd
45–55 Fairchild Street
Heatherton Victoria 3202 Australia
www.hinkler.com.au

BONNEY
PRESS

© Hinkler Books Pty Ltd 2012, 2014

Author: Paula Knight
Illustrator: Guiliano Ferri
Prepress: Graphic Print Group

ISBN: 978 1 7436 3498 1

Printed and bound in China

It Takes Two to T'wit T'woo

Paula Knight • Guiliano Ferri

BONNEY PRESS

Olive Owl could only say 't'wit'.

"T'wit, t'wit," she went. She couldn't say 't'woo'.

She dearly wished to meet another owl who could hoot 't'woo', so that they could 't'wit t'woo' together.

Olive perched high up in her tree and called out,
"T'wit... T'wit..."

She listened carefully with her pointy ears.

"Ribbit... Ribbit..." came the reply.

"Who's there?" said Olive.

"I don't suppose 'ribbit' will do?" asked the frog.

"No, 'ribbit' will never do," said Olive.

She really needed a 't'woo' to go with her 't'wit'.

"T'wit... T'wit... T'wit..." called Olive, trying again.

Her pointy ears were pricked, listening carefully.

"Quack, quack! Quack, quack!" came the reply.

"Who's there?" said Olive.

"I don't suppose a 'quack' will do?" asked the duck.

"I'm sorry," said Olive, sadly. She was hoping for a 't'woo'.

This time, Olive shouted, **"T'wit!"** a bit louder, hoping that somewhere, someone with a lovely 't'woo' might hear her.

"GRRRRRRRRR," came the reply.

"Who's there?" called Olive.

"I don't suppose a 'grrrrrr' will do?" asked the great big grizzly bear.

Olive sighed, "No, not at all, I'm afraid."

What she really wanted was a hooty tooty 't'woo'!

"T'wit... T'wit... T'wit, t'wit, t'wit, t'wit, t'wit!"

This time, Olive carried on 't'witting' over and over again, hoping that her dream owl would surely hear her.

"Anyone there?" she called out.

Before long, new friends surrounded Olive. Everyone had heard her 't'wits', and had come to find out what all the fuss was about. Everyone, that was, apart from Albert.

Albert lived far away, in another tree, in another wood, over the hill.

"T'WOO," he tooted. But nobody could hear him. What Albert wanted more than ever, was a 't'wit' to go with his 't'woo'.

Somewhere in the distance, he thought he could hear a terrible din of quacking, oinking, growling, croaking, hissing, meowing, buzzing, squeaking and woofing. And the odd hee-haw...

Hee-haw

Meow

Squeak Quack

Oink

Croak

Buzz

GROWl

Woof

Hisss

Olive looked down at the duck, the cat, the donkey,
the frog, the dog, the snake, the bee, the pig, the mouse
and the great big grizzly bear.

"What will you do if you can't find a 't'woo'?"
they asked.

"I don't know. Please can you help me?" said Olive.

Together, they all took a huge deep breath...

"T'wi-i-i-t!"

they shouted at the
tops of their voices.

They hushed and listened for a reply. Sure enough, from a far-away wood over the hill, someone had heard them…

"T'woo... T'woo-hoo!" hooted Albert, hardly able to believe what he was hearing.

"T'wi-i-i-t!"

There it was again!

Albert was excited and set off in the direction of the 't'wit', calling, **"T'WOOO!"** as he flew.

"**Woohoo!** I heard it, I really heard it!" said Olive, her feathers all a-fluster.

Albert landed on the tree, right next to her.
They had found each other at last.

"T'woo!" he said.

"T'wit!" said Olive.

"GRRRRR," said the great big grizzly bear.
"That's the wrong way round!"

"T'wit... T'woo!" said Olive and Albert, one after the other.

The animals cheered. Olive and Albert continued 't'witting' and 't'wooing' together until dawn, when they snuggled up for a well-earned sleep.

Many people hear 't'wit, t'woo' and don't know that it takes two owls to make the sound: the female calls 't'wit' and the male answers with 't'woo'.

Tawny owls build their nests in holes in trees. They can only see as well as we do at night, but they use their extra sensitive ears to hunt for food.

Once a couple, tawny owls usually stay together for life.